# The Six Fingers

CW00520301

R. A. Lafferty

**Alpha Editions**

This edition published in 2023

ISBN : 9789357957526

Design and Setting By
**Alpha Editions**
www.alphaedis.com
Email - info@alphaedis.com

# The Six Fingers of Time

*Time is money.*
*Time heals all wounds*
*.Given time,*
*anything is possible.*
*And now he had all the*
*time in the world!*

### By R. A. LAFFERTY
Illustrated by GAUGHAN

HE BEGAN by breaking things that morning. He broke the glass of water on his night stand. He knocked it crazily against the opposite wall and shattered it. Yet it shattered slowly. This would have surprised him if he had been fully awake, for he had only reached out sleepily for it.

Nor had he wakened regularly to his alarm; he had wakened to a weird, slow, low booming, yet the clock said six, time for the alarm. And the low boom, when it came again, seemed to come from the clock.

He reached out and touched it gently, but it floated off the stand at his touch and bounced around slowly on the floor. And when he picked it up again it had stopped, nor would shaking start it.

He checked the electric clock in the kitchen. This also said six o'clock, but the sweep hand did not move. In his living room the radio clock said six, but the second hand seemed stationary.

"But the lights in both rooms work," said Vincent. "How are the clocks stopped? Are they on a separate circuit?"

He went back to his bedroom and got his wristwatch. It also said six; and its sweep hand did not sweep.

"Now this could get silly. What is it that would stop both mechanical and electrical clocks?"

He went to the window and looked out at the clock on the Mutual Insurance Building. It said six o'clock, and the second hand did not move.

- 1 -

"Well, it is possible that the confusion is not limited to myself. I once heard the fanciful theory that a cold shower will clear the mind. For me it never has, but I will try it. I can always use cleanliness for an excuse."

The shower didn't work. Yes, it did: the water came now, but not like water; like very slow syrup that hung in the air. He reached up to touch it there hanging down and stretching. And it shattered like glass when he touched it and drifted in fantastic slow globs across the room. But it had the feel of water, wet and pleasantly cool. And in a quarter of a minute or so it was down over his shoulders and back, and he luxuriated in it. He let it soak his head and it cleared his wits at once.

"There is not a thing wrong with me. I am fine. It is not my fault that the water is slow this morning and other things awry."

He reached for the towel and it tore to pieces in his hands like porous wet paper.

NOW he became very careful in the way he handled things. Slowly, tenderly, and deftly he took them so that they would not break. He shaved himself without mishap in spite of the slow water in the lavatory also.

Then he dressed himself with the greatest caution and cunning, breaking nothing except his shoe laces, a thing that is likely to happen at any time.

"If there is nothing the matter with me, then I will check and see if there is anything seriously wrong with the world. The dawn was fairly along when I looked out, as it should have been. Approximately twenty minutes have passed; it is a clear morning; the sun should now have hit the top several stories of the Insurance Building."

But it had not. It was a clear morning, but the dawn had not brightened at all in the twenty minutes. And that big clock still said six. It had not changed.

Yet it had changed, and he knew it with a queer feeling. He pictured it as it had been before. The hour and the minute hand had not moved noticeably. But the second hand had moved. It had moved a third of the dial.

So he pulled up a chair to the window and watched it. He realized that, though he could not see it move, yet it did make progress. He watched it for perhaps five minutes. It moved through a space of perhaps five seconds.

"Well, that is not my problem. It is that of the clock maker, either a terrestrial or a celestial one."

But he left his rooms without a good breakfast, and he left them very early. How did he know that it was early since there was something wrong with the time? Well, it was early at least according to the sun and according to the clocks, neither of which institutions seemed to be working properly.

He left without a good breakfast because the coffee would not make and the bacon would not fry. And in plain point of fact the fire would not heat. The gas flame came from the pilot light like a slowly spreading stream or an unfolding flower. Then it burned far too steadily. The skillet remained cold when placed over it; nor would water even heat. It had taken at least five minutes to get the water out of the faucet in the first place.

He ate a few pieces of leftover bread and some scraps of meat.

In the street there was no motion, no real motion. A truck, first seeming at rest, moved very slowly. There was no gear in which it could move so slowly. And there was a taxi which crept along, but Charles Vincent had to look at it carefully for some time to be sure that it was in motion. Then he received a shock. He realized by the early morning light that the driver of it was dead. Dead with his eyes wide open!

Slowly as it was going, and by whatever means it was moving, it should really be stopped. He walked over to it, opened the door, and pulled on the brake. Then he looked into the eyes of the dead man. Was he really dead? It was hard to be sure. He felt warm. But, even as Vincent looked, the eyes of the dead man had begun to close. And close they did and open again in a matter of about twenty seconds.

THIS was weird. The slowly closing and opening eyes sent a chill through Vincent. And the dead man had begun to lean forward in his seat. Vincent put a hand in the middle of the man's chest to hold him upright, but he found the forward pressure as relentless as it was slow. He was unable to keep the dead man up.

So he let him go, watching curiously; and in a few seconds the driver's face was against the wheel. But it was almost as if it had no intention of stopping there. It pressed into the wheel with dogged force. He would surely break his face. Vincent took several holds on the dead man and counteracted the pressure somewhat. Yet the face was being damaged, and if things were normal, blood would have flowed.

The man had been dead so long however, that (though he was still warm) his blood must have congealed, for it was fully two minutes before it began to ooze.

"Whatever I have done, I have done enough damage," said Vincent. "And, in whatever nightmare I am in, I am likely to do further harm if I meddle more. I had better leave it alone."

He walked on down the morning street. Yet whatever vehicles he saw were moving with an incredible slowness, as though driven by some fantastic gear reduction. And there were people here and there frozen solid. It was a chilly morning, but it was not that cold. They were immobile in positions of motion, as though they were playing the children's game of Statues.

"How is it," said Charles Vincent, "that this young girl (who I believe works across the street from us) should have died standing up and in full stride? But, no. She is not dead. Or, if so, she died with a very alert expression. And—oh, my God, she's doing it too!"

For he realized that the eyes of the girl were closing, and in the space of no more than a quarter of a second they had completed their cycle and were open again. Also, and this was even stranger, she had moved, moved forward in full stride. He would have timed her if he could, but how could he when all the clocks were crazy? Yet she must have been taking about two steps a minute.

He went into the cafeteria. The early morning crowd that he had often watched through the windows was there. The girl who made flapjacks in the window had just flipped one and it hung in the air. Then it floated over as if caught by a slight breeze, and sank slowly down as if settling in water.

The breakfasters, like the people in the street, were all dead in this new way, moving with almost imperceptible motion. And all had apparently died in the act of drinking coffee, eating eggs, or munching toast. And if there were only time enough, there was even a chance that they would get the drinking, eating, and munching done with, for there was the shadow of movement in them all.

The cashier had the register drawer open and money in her hand, and the hand of the customer was outstretched for it. In time, somewhere in the new leisurely time, the hands would come together and the change be given. And so it happened. It may have been a minute and a half, or two minutes, or two and a half. It is always hard to judge time, and now it had become all but impossible.

"I am still hungry," said Charles Vincent, "but it would be foolhardy to wait for service here. Should I help myself? They will not mind if they are dead. And if they are not dead, in any case it seems that I am invisible to them."

HE WOLFED several rolls. He opened a bottle of milk and held it upside down over his glass while he ate another roll. Liquids had all become perversely slow.

But he felt better for his erratic breakfast. He would have paid for it, but how?

He left the cafeteria and walked about the town as it seemed still to be quite early, though one could depend on neither sun nor clock for the time any more. The traffic lights were unchanging. He sat for a long time in a little park and watched the town and the big clock in the Commerce Building tower; but like all the clocks it was either stopped or the hand would creep too slowly to be seen.

It must have been just about an hour till the traffic lights changed, but change they did at last. By picking a point on the building across the street and watching what moved past it, he found that the traffic did indeed move. In a minute or so, the entire length of a car would pass the given point.

He had, he recalled, been very far behind in his work and it had been worrying him. He decided to go to the office, early as it was or seemed to be.

He let himself in. Nobody else was there. He resolved not to look at the clock and to be very careful of the way he handled all objects because of his new propensity for breaking things. This considered, all seemed normal there. He had said the day before that he could hardly catch up on his work if he put in two days solid. He now resolved at least to work steadily until something happened, whatever it was.

For hour after hour he worked on his tabulations and reports. Nobody else had arrived. Could something be wrong? Certainly something was wrong. But this was not a holiday. That was not it.

Just how long can a stubborn and mystified man plug away at his task? It was hour after hour after hour. He did not become hungry nor particularly tired. And he did get through a lot of work.

"It must be half done. However it has happened, I have caught up on at least a day's work. I will keep on."

He must have continued silently for another eight or ten hours.

He was caught up completely on his back work.

"Well, to some extent I can work into the future. I can head up and carry over. I can put in everything but the figures of the field reports."

And he did so.

"It will be hard to bury me in work again. I could almost coast for a day. I don't even know what day it is, but I must have worked twenty hours straight through and nobody has arrived. Perhaps nobody ever will arrive. If they are moving with the speed of the people in the nightmare outside, it is no wonder they have not arrived."

He put his head down on his arms on the desk. The last thing he saw before he closed his eyes was the misshapen left thumb that he had always tried to conceal a little by the way he handled his hands.

"At least I know that I am still myself. I'd know myself anywhere by that."

Then he went to sleep at his desk.

JENNY came in with a quick click-click-click of high heels, and he wakened to the noise.

"What are you doing dozing at your desk, Mr. Vincent? Have you been here all night?"

"I don't know, Jenny. Honestly I don't."

"I was only teasing. Sometimes when I get here a little early I take a catnap myself."

The clock said six minutes till eight and the second hand was sweeping normally. Time had returned to the world. Or to him. But had all that early morning of his been a dream? Then it had been a very efficient dream. He had accomplished work that he could hardly have done in two days. And it was the same day that it was supposed to be.

He went to the water fountain. The water now behaved normally. He went to the window. The traffic was behaving as it should. Though sometimes slow and sometimes snarled, yet it was in the pace of the regular world.

The other workers arrived. They were not balls of fire, but neither was it necessary to observe them for several minutes to be sure they weren't dead.

"It did have its advantages," Charles Vincent said. "I would be afraid to live with it permanently, but it would be handy to go into for a few minutes a day and accomplish the business of hours. I may be a case for the doctor. But just how would I go about telling a doctor what was bothering me?"

Now it had surely been less than two hours from his first rising till the time that he wakened to the noise of Jenny from his second sleep. And how long that second sleep had been, or in which time enclave, he had no idea. But how account for it all? He had spent a long while in his own rooms, much longer than ordinary in his confusion. He had walked the city mile after mile in his puzzlement. And he had sat in the little park for hours and studied the situation. And he had worked at his own desk for an outlandish long time.

Well, he would go to the doctor. A man is obliged to refrain from making a fool of himself to the world at large, but to his own lawyer, his priest, or his doctor he will sometimes have to come as a fool. By their callings they are restrained from scoffing openly.

Dr. Mason was not particularly a friend. Charles Vincent realized with some unease that he did not have any particular friends, only acquaintances and associates. It was as though he were of a species slightly apart from his fellows. He wished now a little that he had a particular friend.

But Dr. Mason was an acquaintance of some years, had the reputation of being a good doctor, and besides Vincent had now arrived at his office and been shown in. He would either have to—well, that was as good a beginning as any.

"Doctor, I am in a predicament. I will either have to invent some symptoms to account for my visit here, or make an excuse and bolt, or tell you what is bothering me, even though you will think I am a new sort of idiot."

"Vincent, every day people invent symptoms to cover their visits here, and I know that they have lost their nerve about the real reason for coming. And every day people do make excuses and bolt. But experience tells me that I will get a larger fee if you tackle the third alternative. And, Vincent, there is no new sort of idiot."

VINCENT said, "It may not sound so silly if I tell it quickly. I awoke this morning to some very puzzling incidents. It seemed that time itself had stopped, or that the whole world had gone into super-slow motion. The water would neither flow nor boil, and fire would not heat food. The clocks, which I first believed had stopped, crept along at perhaps a minute an hour. The people I met in the streets appeared dead, frozen in lifelike attitudes. And it was only by watching them for a very long time that I perceived that they did indeed have motion. One car I saw creeping slower than the most backward snail, and a dead man at the wheel of it. I went to it, opened the door, and put on the brake. I realized after a time that the man was not dead. But he bent forward and broke his face on the steering wheel. It must have taken a full minute for his head to travel no more than ten inches, yet I was unable to prevent his hitting the wheel. I then did other bizarre things in a world that had died on its feet. I walked many miles through the city, and then I sat for hours in the park. I went to the office and let myself in. I accomplished work that must have taken me twenty hours. I then took a nap at my desk. When I awoke on the arrival of the others, it was six minutes to eight in the morning of the same day, today. Not two hours had passed from my rising, and time was back to normal. But the things that happened in that time that could never be compressed into two hours."

"One question first, Vincent. Did you actually accomplish the work of many hours?"

"I did. It was done, and done in that time. It did not become undone on the return of time to normal."

"A second question. Had you been worried about your work, about being behind?"

"Yes. Emphatically."

"Then here is one explanation. You retired last night. But very shortly afterward you arose in a state of somnambulism. There are facets of sleepwalking which we do not at all understand. The time-out-of-focus interludes were parts of a walking dream of yours. You dressed and went to your office and worked all night. It is possible to do routine tasks in a somnambulistic state rapidly and even feverishly, with an intense concentration—to perform prodigies. You may have fallen into a normal sleep there when you had finished, or you may have been awakened directly from your somnambulistic trance on the arrival of your co-workers. There, that is a plausible and workable explanation. In the case of an apparently bizarre happening, it is always well to have a rational explanation to fall back on. They will usually satisfy a patient and put his mind at rest. But often they do not satisfy me."

"Your explanation very nearly satisfies me, Dr. Mason, and it does put my mind considerably at rest. I am sure that in a short while I will be able to accept it completely. But why does it not satisfy you?"

"One reason is a man I treated early this morning. He had his face smashed, and he had seen—or almost seen—a ghost: a ghost of incredible swiftness that was more sensed than seen. The ghost opened the door of his car while it was going at full speed, jerked on the brake, and caused him to crack his head. This man was dazed and had a slight concussion. I have convinced him that he did not see any ghost at all, that he must have dozed at the wheel and run into something. As I say, I am harder to convince than my patients. But it may have been coincidence."

"I hope so. But you also seem to have another reservation."

"After quite a few years in practice, I seldom see or hear anything new. Twice before I have been told a happening or a dream on the line of what you experienced."

"Did you convince your patients that it was only a dream?"

"I did. Both of them. That is, I convinced them the first few times it happened to them."

"Were they satisfied?"

"At first. Later, not entirely. But they both died within a year of their first coming to me."

"Nothing violent, I hope."

"Both had the gentlest deaths. That of senility extreme."

"Oh. Well, I'm too young for that."

"I would like you to come back in a month or so."

"I will, if the delusion or the dream returns. Or if I do not feel well."

After this Charles Vincent began to forget about the incident. He only recalled it with humor sometimes when again he was behind in his work.

"Well, if it gets bad enough I may do another sleepwalking act and catch up. But if there is another aspect of time and I could enter it at will, it might often be handy."

CHARLES VINCENT never saw his face at all. It is very dark in some of those clubs and the Coq Bleu is like the inside of a tomb. He went to the clubs only about once a month, sometimes after a show when he did not want to go home to bed, sometimes when he was just plain restless.

Citizens of the more fortunate states may not know of the mysteries of the clubs. In Vincent's the only bars are beer bars, and only in the clubs can a person get a drink, and only members are admitted. It is true that even such a small club as the Coq Bleu had thirty thousand members, and at a dollar a year that is a nice sideline. The little numbered membership cards cost a penny each for the printing, and the member wrote in his own name. But he had to have a card—or a dollar for a card—to gain admittance.

But there could be no entertainments in the clubs. There was nothing there but the little bar room in the near darkness.

The man was there, and then he was not, and then he was there again. And always where he sat it was too dark to see his face.

"I wonder," he said to Vincent (or to the bar at large, though there were no other customers and the bartender was asleep), "I wonder if you have ever read Zurbarin on the Relationship of Extradigitalism to Genius?"

"I have never heard of the work nor of the man," said Vincent. "I doubt if either exists."

"I am Zurbarin," said the man.

Vincent hid his misshapen left thumb. Yet it could not have been noticed in that light, and he must have been crazy to believe there was any connection between it and the man's remark. It was not truly a double thumb. He was not an extradigital, nor was he a genius.

"I refuse to become interested in you," said Vincent. "I am on the verge of leaving. I dislike waking the bartender, but I did want another drink."

"Sooner done than said."

"What is?"

"Your glass is full."

"It is? So it is. Is it a trick?"

"Trick is the name for anything either too frivolous or too mystifying for us to comprehend. But on one long early morning of a month ago, you also could have done the trick, and nearly as well."

"Could I have? How would you know about my long early morning—assuming there to have been such?"

"I watched you for a while. Few others have the equipment to watch you with when you're in the aspect."

SO THEY were silent for some time, and Vincent watched the clock and was ready to go.

"I wonder," said the man in the dark, "if you have read Schimmelpenninck on the Sexagintal and the Duodecimal in the Chaldee Mysteries?"

"I have not and I doubt if anyone else has. I would guess that you are also Schimmelpenninck and that you have just made up the name on the spur of the moment."

"I am Schimm, it is true, but I made up the name on the spur of a moment many years ago."

"I am a little bored with you," said Vincent, "but I would appreciate it if you'd do your glass-filling trick once more."

"I have just done so. And you are not bored; you are frightened."

"Of what?" asked Vincent, whose glass was in fact full again.

"Of reentering a dread that you are not sure was a dream. But there are advantages to being both invisible and inaudible."

"Can you be invisible?"

"Was I not when I went behind the bar just now and fixed you a drink?"

"How?"

"A man in full stride goes at the rate of about five miles an hour. Multiply that by sixty, which is the number of time. When I leave my stool and go behind the bar, I go and return at the rate of three hundred miles an hour. So I am invisible to you, particularly if I move while you blink."

"One thing does not match. You might have got around there and back, but you could not have poured."

"Shall I say that mastery over liquids is not given to beginners? But for us there are many ways to outwit the slowness of matter."

"I believe that you are a hoaxer. Do you know Dr. Mason?"

"I know that you went to see him. I know of his futile attempts to penetrate a certain mystery. But I have not talked to him of you."

"I still believe that you are a phony. Could you put me back into the state of my dream of a month ago?"

"It was not a dream. But I could put you again into that state."

"Prove it."

"Watch the clock. Do you believe that I can point my finger at it and stop it for you? It is already stopped for me."

"No, I don't believe it. Yes, I guess I have to, since I see that you have just done it. But it may be another trick. I don't know where the clock is plugged in."

"Neither do I. Come to the door. Look at every clock you can see. Are they not all stopped?"

"Yes. Maybe the power has gone off all over town."

"You know it has not. There are still lighted windows in those buildings, though it is quite late."

"Why are you playing with me? I am neither on the inside nor the outside. Either tell me the secret or say that you will not tell me."

"The secret isn't a simple one. It can only be arrived at after all philosophy and learning have been assimilated."

"One man cannot arrive at that in one lifetime."

"Not in an ordinary lifetime. But the secret of the secret (if I may put it that way) is that one must use part of it as a tool in learning. You could not learn all in one lifetime, but by being permitted the first step—to be able to read, say, sixty books in the time it took you to read one, to pause for a minute in thought and use up only one second, to get a day's work accomplished in eight minutes and so have time for other things—by such ways one may make a beginning. I will warn you, though. Even for the most intelligent, it is a race."

"A race? What race?"

"It is a race between success, which is life, and failure, which is death."

"Let's skip the melodrama. How do I get into the state and out of it?"

"Oh, that is simple, so easy that it seems like a gadget. Here are two diagrams I will draw. Note them carefully. This first, envision it in your mind and you are in the state. Now this second one, envision, and you are out of it."

"That easy?"

"That deceptively easy. The trick is to learn why it works—if you want to succeed, meaning to live."

So Charles Vincent left him and went home, walking the mile in a little less than fifteen normal seconds. But he still had not seen the face of the man.

THERE are advantages intellectual, monetary, and amorous in being able to enter the accelerated state at will. It is a fox game. One must be careful not to be caught at it, nor to break or harm that which is in the normal state.

Vincent could always find eight or ten minutes unobserved to accomplish the day's work. And a fifteen-minute coffee break could turn into a fifteen-hour romp around the town.

There was this boyish pleasure in becoming a ghost: to appear and stand motionless in front of an onrushing train and to cause the scream of the whistle, and to be in no danger, being able to move five or ten times as fast as the train; to enter and to sit suddenly in the middle of a select group and see them stare, and then disappear from the middle of them; to interfere in sports and games, entering a prize ring and tripping, hampering, or slugging the unliked fighter; to blue-shot down the hockey ice, skating at fifteen hundred miles an hour and scoring dozens of goals at either end while the people only know that something odd is happening.

There was pleasure in being able to shatter windows by chanting little songs, for the voice (when in the state) will be to the world at sixty times its regular pitch, though normal to oneself. And for this reason also he was inaudible to others.

There was fun in petty thieving and tricks. He would take a wallet from a man's pocket and be two blocks away when the victim turned at the feel. He would come back and stuff it into the man's mouth as he bleated to a policeman.

He would come into the home of a lady writing a letter, snatch up the paper and write three lines and vanish before the scream got out of her throat.

He would take food off forks, put baby turtles and live fish into bowls of soup between spoonfuls of the eater.

He would lash the hands of handshakers tightly together with stout cord. He unzipped persons of both sexes when they were at their most pompous. He changed cards from one player's hand to another's. He removed golf balls from tees during the backswing and left notes written large "YOU MISSED ME" pinned to the ground with the tee.

Or he shaved mustaches and heads. Returning repeatedly to one woman he disliked, he gradually clipped her bald and finally gilded her pate.

With tellers counting their money, he interfered outrageously and enriched himself. He snipped cigarettes in two with a scissors and blew out matches, so that one frustrated man broke down and cried at his inability to get a light.

He removed the weapons from the holsters of policemen and put cap pistols and water guns in their places. He unclipped the leashes of dogs and substituted little toy dogs rolling on wheels.

He put frogs in water glasses and left lighted firecrackers on bridge tables.

He reset wrist watches on wrists, and played pranks in men's rooms.

"I was always a boy at heart," said Charles Vincent.

ALSO during those first few days of the controlled new state, he established himself materially, acquiring wealth by devious ways, and opening bank accounts in various cities under various names, against a time of possible need.

Nor did he ever feel any shame for the tricks he played on unaccelerated humanity. For the people, when he was in the state, were as statues to him, hardly living, barely moving, unseeing, unhearing. And it is no shame to show disrespect to such comical statues.

And also, and again because he was a boy at heart, he had fun with the girls.

"I am one mass of black and blue marks," said Jenny one day. "My lips are sore and my front teeth feel loosened. I don't know what in the world is the matter with me."

Yet he had not meant to bruise or harm her. He was rather fond of her and he resolved to be much more careful. Yet it was fun, when he was in the state and invisible to her because of his speed, to kiss her here and there in out-of-the-way places. She made a nice statue and it was good sport. And there were others.

"You look older," said one of his co-workers one day. "Are you taking care of yourself? Are you worried?"

"I am not," said Vincent. "I never felt better or happier in my life."

But now there was time for so many things—time, in fact, for everything. There was no reason why he could not master anything in the world, when he could take off for fifteen minutes and gain fifteen hours. Vincent was a rapid but careful reader. He could now read from a hundred and twenty to two hundred books in an evening and night; and he slept in the accelerated state and could get a full night's sleep in eight minutes.

He first acquired a knowledge of languages. A quite extensive reading knowledge of a language can be acquired in three hundred hours world time, or three hundred minutes (five hours) accelerated time. And if one takes the tongues in order, from the most familiar to the most remote, there is no real difficulty. He acquired fifty for a starter, and could always add any other any evening that he found he had a need for it. And at the same time he began to assemble and consolidate knowledge. Of literature, properly speaking, there are no more than ten thousand books that are really worth reading and falling in love with. These were gone through with high pleasure, and two or three thousand of them were important enough to be reserved for future rereading.

History, however, is very uneven; and it is necessary to read texts and sources that for form are not worth reading. And the same with philosophy. Mathematics and science, pure or physical, could not, of course, be covered with the same speed. Yet, with time available, all could be mastered. There is no concept ever expressed by any human mind that cannot be comprehended by any other normal human mind, if time is available and it is taken in the proper order and context and with the proper preparatory work.

And often, and now more often, Vincent felt that he was touching the fingers of the secret; and always, when he came near it, it had a little bit the smell of the pit.

For he had pegged out all the main points of the history of man; or rather most of the tenable, or at least possible, theories of the history of man. It was hard to hold the main line of it, that double road of rationality and revelation that should lead always to a fuller and fuller development (not the fetish of progress, that toy word used only by toy people), to an unfolding and growth and perfectibility.

But the main line was often obscure and all but obliterated, and traced through fog and miasma. He had accepted the Fall of Man and the Redemption as the cardinal points of history. But he understood now that neither happened only once, that both were of constant occurrence; that there was a hand reaching up from that old pit with its shadow over man. And he had come to picture that hand in his dreams (for his dreams were especially vivid when in the state) as a six-digited monster reaching out. He began to realize that the thing he was caught in was dangerous and deadly.

Very dangerous.

Very deadly.

One of the weird books that he often returned to and which continually puzzled him was the Relationship of Extradigitalism to Genius, written by the man whose face he had never seen, in one of his manifestations.

It promised more than it delivered, and it intimated more than it said. Its theory was tedious and tenuous, bolstered with undigested mountains of doubtful data. It left him unconvinced that persons of genius (even if it could be agreed who or what they were) had often the oddity of extra fingers and toes, or the vestiges of them. And it puzzled him what possible difference it could make.

YET there were hints here of a Corsican who commonly kept a hand hidden, or an earlier and more bizarre commander who wore always a mailed glove, of another man with a glove between the two; hints that the multiplex-adept, Leonardo himself, who sometimes drew the hands of men and often those of monsters with six fingers, may himself have had the touch. There was a comment of Caesar, not conclusive, to the same effect.

It is known that Alexander had a minor peculiarity; it is not known what it was; this man made it seem that this was it. And it was averred of Gregory and Augustine, of Benedict and Albert and Acquinas. Yet a man with a deformity could not enter the priesthood; if they had it, it must have been in vestigial form.

There were cases for Charles Magnut and Mahmud, for Saladin the Horseman and for Akhnaton the King; for Homer (a Seleuciad-Greek statuette shows him with six fingers strumming an unidentified instrument while reciting); for Pythagoras, for Buonarroti, Santi, Theotokopolous, van Rijn, Robusti.

Zurbarin catalogued eight thousand names. He maintained that they were geniuses. And that they were extradigitals.

Charles Vincent grinned and looked down at his misshapen or double thumb.

"At least I am in good though monotonous company. But what in the name of triple time is he driving at?"

And it was not long afterward that Vincent was examining cuneiform tablets in the State Museum. These were a broken and not continuous series on the theory of numbers, tolerably legible to the now encyclopedic Charles Vincent. And the series read in part:

"On the divergence of the basis itself and the confusion caused—for it is five, or it is six, or ten or twelve, or sixty or a hundred, or three hundred and sixty or the double hundred, the thousand. The reason, not clearly understood by the people, is that Six and the Dozen are first, and Sixty is a compromise in condescending to the people. For the five, the ten are late, and are no older than the people themselves. It is said, and credited, that people began to count by fives and tens from the number of fingers on their hands. But before the people the—by the reason that they had—counted by sixes and twelves. But Sixty is the number of time, divisible by both, for both must live together in time, though not on the same plane of time—" Much of the rest was scattered. And it was while trying to set the hundreds of unordered clay tablets in proper sequence that Charles Vincent created the legend of the ghost in the museum.

For he spent his multi-hundred-hour nights there studying and classifying. Naturally he could not work without light, and naturally he could be seen when he sat still at his studies. But as the slow-moving guards attempted to close in on him, he would move to avoid them, and his speed made him invisible to them. They were a nuisance and had to be discouraged. He belabored them soundly and they became less eager to try to capture him.

His only fear was that they would some time try to shoot him to see if he were ghost or human. He could avoid a seen shot, which would come at no more than two and a half times his own greatest speed. But an unperceived shot could penetrate dangerously, even fatally, before he twisted away from it.

He had fathered legends of other ghosts, that of the Central Library, that of University Library, that of the John Charles Underwood Jr. Technical Library. This plurality of ghosts tended to cancel out each other and bring believers into ridicule. Even those who had seen him as a ghost did not admit that they believed in the ghosts.

HE WENT back to Dr. Mason for his monthly checkup.

"You look terrible," said the Doctor. "Whatever it is, you have changed. If you can afford it, you should take a long rest."

"I have the means," said Charles Vincent, "and that is just what I will do. I'll take a rest for a year or two."

He had begun to begrudge the time that he must spend at the world's pace. From now on he was regarded as a recluse. He was silent and unsociable, for he found it a nuisance to come back to the common state to engage in conversation, and in his special state voices were too slow-pitched to intrude into his consciousness.

Except that of the man whose face he had never seen.

"You are making very tardy progress," said the man. Once more they were in a dark club. "Those who do not show more progress we cannot use. After all, you are only a vestigial. It is probable that you have very little of the ancient race in you. Fortunately those who do not show progress destroy themselves. You had not imagined that there were only two phases of time, had you?"

"Lately I have come to suspect that there are many more," said Charles Vincent.

"And you understand that only one step cannot succeed?"

"I understand that the life I have been living is in direct violation of all that we know of the laws of mass, momentum, and acceleration, as well as those of conservation of energy, the potential of the human person, the moral compensation, the golden mean, and the capacity of human organs. I know that I cannot multiply energy and experience sixty times without a compensating increase of food intake, and yet I do it. I know that I cannot live on eight minutes' sleep in twenty-four hours, but I do that also. I know that I cannot reasonably crowd four thousand years of experience into one lifetime, yet unreasonably I do not see what will prevent it. But you say I will destroy myself."

"Those who take only the first step destroy themselves."

"And how does one take the second step?"

"At the proper moment you will be given the choice."

"I have the most uncanny feeling that I will refuse the choice."

"From present indications, you will refuse it. You are fastidious."

"You have a smell about you, Old Man without a face. I know now what it is. It is the smell of the pit."

"Are you so slow to learn that?"

"It is the mud from the pit, the same from which the clay tablets were formed, from the old land between the rivers. I've dreamed of the six-fingered hand reaching up from the pit and overshadowing us all. And I have read: 'The people first counted by fives and tens from the number of fingers on their hands. But before the people—for the reason that they had—counted by sixes and twelves.' But time has left blanks in those tablets."

"Yes, time in one of its manifestations has deftly and with a purpose left those blanks."

"I cannot discover the name of the thing that goes in one of those blanks. Can you?"

"I am part of the name that goes into one of those blanks."

"And you are the man without a face. But why is it that you overshadow and control people? And to what purpose?"

"It will be long before you know those answers."

"When the choice comes to me, it will bear very careful weighing."

AFTER that a chill descended on the life of Charles Vincent, for all that he still possessed his exceptional powers. And he seldom now indulged in pranks.

Except for Jennifer Parkey.

It was unusual that he should be drawn to her. He knew her only slightly in the common world and she was at least fifteen years his senior. But now she appealed to him for her youthful qualities, and all his pranks with her were gentle ones.

For one thing this spinster did not frighten, nor did she begin locking her doors, never having bothered about such things before. He would come behind her and stroke her hair, and she would speak out calmly with that sort of quickening in her voice: "Who are you? Why won't you let me see you? You are a friend, aren't you? Are you a man, or are you something else? If you can caress me, why can't you talk to me? Please let me see you. I promise that I won't hurt you."

It was as though she could not imagine that anything strange would hurt her. Or again when he hugged her or kissed her on the nape, she would call: "You must be a little boy, or very like a little boy, whoever you are. You are good not to break my things when you move about. Come here and let me hold you."

It is only very good people who have no fear at all of the unknown.

When Vincent met Jennifer in the regular world, as he more often now found occasion to do, she looked at him appraisingly, as though she guessed some sort of connection.

She said one day: "I know it is an impolite thing to say, but you do not look well at all. Have you been to a doctor?"

"Several times. But I think it is my doctor who should go to a doctor. He was always given to peculiar remarks, but now he is becoming a little unsettled."

"If I were your doctor, I believe I would also become a little unsettled. But you should find out what is wrong. You look terrible."

He did not look terrible. He had lost his hair, it is true, but many men lose their hair by thirty, though not perhaps as suddenly as he had. He thought of attributing it to the air resistance. After all, when he was in the state he did stride at some three hundred miles an hour. And enough of that is likely to blow the hair right off your head. And might that not also be the reason for his worsened complexion and the tireder look that appeared in his eyes? But he knew that this was nonsense. He felt no more air pressure when in his accelerated state than when in the normal one.

He had received his summons. He chose not to answer it. He did not want to be presented with the choice; he had no wish to be one with those of the pit. But he had no intention of giving up the great advantage which he now held over nature.

"I will have it both ways," he said. "I am already a contradiction and an impossibility. The proverb was only the early statement of the law of moral compensation: 'You can't take more out of a basket than it holds.' But for a long time I have been in violation of the laws and balances. 'There is no road without a turning,' 'Those who dance will have to pay the fiddler,' 'Everything that goes up comes down,' But are proverbs really universal laws? Certainly. A sound proverb has the force of universal law; it is but another statement of it. But I have contradicted the universal laws. It remains to be seen whether I have contradicted them with impunity. 'Every action has its reaction.' If I refuse to deal with them, I will provoke a strong reaction. The man without a face said that it was always a race between full knowing and destruction. Very well, I will race them for it."

THEY began to persecute him then. He knew that they were in a state as accelerated from his as his was from the normal. To them he was the almost motionless statue, hardly to be told from a dead man. To him they were by their speed both invisible and inaudible. They hurt him and haunted him. But still he would not answer the summons.

When the meeting took place, it was they who had to come to him, and they materialized there in his room, men without faces.

"The choice," said one. "You force us to be so clumsy as to have to voice it."

"I will have no part of you. You all smell of the pit, of that old mud of the cuneiforms of the land between the rivers, of the people who were before the people."

"It has endured a long time, and we consider it as enduring forever. But the Garden which was in the neighborhood—do you know how long the Garden lasted?"

"I don't know."

"That all happened in a single day, and before nightfall they were outside. You want to throw in with something more permanent, don't you."

"No. I don't believe I do."

"What have you to lose?"

"Only my hope of eternity."

"But you don't believe in that. No man has ever really believed in eternity."

"No man has ever either entirely believed or disbelieved in it," said Charles Vincent.

"At least it cannot be proved," said one of the faceless men. "Nothing is proved until it is over with. And in this case, if it is ever over with, then it is disproved. And all that time would one not be tempted to wonder, 'What if, after all, it ends in the next minute?'"

"I imagine that if we survive the flesh we will receive some sort of surety," said Vincent.

"But you are not sure either of such surviving or receiving. Now *we* have a very close approximation of eternity. When time is multiplied by itself, and that repeated again and again, does that not approximate eternity?"

"I don't believe it does. But I will not be of you. One of you has said that I am too fastidious. So now will you say that you'll destroy me?"

"No. We will only let you be destroyed. By yourself, you cannot win the race with destruction."

After that Charles Vincent somehow felt more mature. He knew he was not really meant to be a six-fingered thing of the pit. He knew that in some way he would have to pay for every minute and hour that he had gained. But what he had gained he would use to the fullest. And whatever could be accomplished by sheer acquisition of human knowledge, he would try to accomplish.

And he now startled Dr. Mason by the medical knowledge he had picked up, the while the doctor amused him by the concern he showed for Vincent. For he felt fine. He was perhaps not as active as he had been, but that was only because he had become dubious of aimless activity. He was still the ghost of the libraries and museums, but was puzzled that the published reports intimated that an old ghost had replaced a young one.

HE NOW paid his mystic visits to Jennifer Parkey less often. For he was always dismayed to hear her exclaim to him in his ghostly form: "Your touch is so changed. You poor thing! Is there anything at all I can do to help you?"

He decided that somehow she was too immature to understand him, though he was still fond of her. He transferred his affections to Mrs. Milly Maltby, a widow at least thirty years his senior. Yet here it was a sort of girlishness in her that appealed to him. She was a woman of sharp wit and real affection, and she also accepted his visitations without fear, following a little initial panic.

They played games, writing games, for they communicated by writing. She would scribble a line, then hold the paper up in the air whence he would cause it to vanish into his sphere. He would return it in half a minute, or half a second by her time, with his retort. He had the advantage of her in time with greatly more opportunity to think up responses, but she had the advantage over him in natural wit and was hard to top.

They also played checkers, and he often had to retire apart and read a chapter of a book on the art between moves, and even so she often beat him; for native talent is likely to be a match for accumulated lore and codified procedure.

But to Milly also he was unfaithful in his fashion, being now interested (he no longer became enamored or entranced) in a Mrs. Roberts, a great-grandmother who was his elder by at least fifty years. He had read all the data extant on the attraction of the old for the young, but he still could not explain his successive attachments. He decided that these three examples were enough to establish a universal law: that a woman is simply not afraid of a ghost, though he touches her and is invisible, and writes her notes without hands. It is possible that amorous spirits have known this for a long time, but Charles Vincent had made the discovery himself independently.

When enough knowledge is accumulated on any subject, the pattern will sometimes emerge suddenly, like a form in a picture revealed where before it was not seen. And when enough knowledge is accumulated on all subjects, is there not a chance that a pattern governing all subjects will emerge?

Charles Vincent was caught up in one last enthusiasm. On a long vigil, as he consulted source after source and sorted them in his mind, it seemed that the pattern was coming out clearly and simply, for all its amazing complexity of detail.

"I know everything that they know in the pit, and I know a secret that they do not know. I have not lost the race—I have won it. I can defeat them at the point where they believe themselves invulnerable. If controlled hereafter, we need at least not be controlled by them. It is all falling together now. I have found the final truth, and it is they who have lost the race. I hold the key. I will now be able to enjoy the advantage without paying the ultimate price of defeat and destruction, or of collaboration with them.

"Now I have only to implement my knowledge, to publish the fact, and one shadow at least will be lifted from mankind. I will do it at once. Well, nearly at once. It is almost dawn in the normal world. I will sit here a very little while and rest. Then I will go out and begin to make contact with the proper persons for the disposition of this thing. But first I will sit here a little while and rest."

And he died quietly in his chair as he sat there.

DR. MASON made an entry in his private journal: "Charles Vincent, a completely authenticated case of premature aging, one of the most clear-cut in all gerontology. This man was known to me for years, and I here aver that as of one year ago he was of normal appearance and physical state, and that his chronology is also correct, I having also known his father. I examined the subject during the period of his illness, and there is no question at all of his identity, which has also been established for the record by fingerprinting and other means. I aver that Charles Vincent at the age of thirty is dead of old age, having the appearance and organic condition of a man of ninety."

Then the doctor began to make another note: "As in two other cases of my own observation, the illness was accompanied by a certain delusion and series of dreams, so nearly identical in the three men as to be almost unbelievable. And for the record, and no doubt to the prejudice of my own reputation, I will set down the report of them here."

But when Dr. Mason had written that, he thought about it for a while.

"No, I will do no such thing," he said, and he struck out the last lines he had written. "It is best to let sleeping dragons lie."

And somewhere the faceless men with the smell of the pit on them smiled to themselves in quiet irony.

**END**

9 789357 957526